Barnaby
NEVER FORGETS

For Kirsten and Dave

First edition 2017

Library of Congress Catalog Card Number pending
ISBN 978-0-7636-8853-0

17 18 19 20 21 22 CCP 10 9 8 7 6 5 4 3 2 1

Printed in Shenzhen, Guangdong, China

This book was typeset in Chowderhead.
The illustrations were created digitally.

Candlewick Press
99 Dover Street
Somerville, Massachusetts 02144

visit us at www.candlewick.com

Barnaby
NEVER FORGETS

Pierre Collet-Derby

CANDLEWICK PRESS

Where

in the world

did I put them?

I'm usually GREAT at remembering things.

I never forget to feed my grasshoppers in the morning.

And I remember to write my letter to Santa every single year.

Hey, there they are!

I found them!

OK, maybe things do slip my mind every now and then.

I forget to hang up my wet bathing suit sometimes.

I guess I don't always remember to wash my hands.

And I may have a few
overdue library books.

Sometimes I even forget what I'm supposed to be doing

or where I put my jacket.

But it can be **FUN** to find things I forgot I had!

Like the dollar bill Grandma gave me for raking the leaves

or my favorite old bunny.

Once, I forgot to put the trash in the garbage can.

What happened next was
IN-CRE-DI-BLE!

And look what I just found in my backpack: a lollipop from my birthday last year!

This is turning out to be
my lucky day!

Hey, wait a second. . . .

I just remembered!

TODAY IS SATURDAY!

See? I don't forget everything!